THE MYSTERIOUS LIVER

BY

MIKE EFFA

Imaginarium Self-Publishing
An Imprint of Copyhouse Press Ltd
International House, 24 Holborn Viaduct
London
United Kingdom, EC1A 2BN

ISBN 978-0993394058

DEDICATION

All glory to God for a dream fulfilled.

To my wonderful son, Asher Effa

The Mysterious Liver

CHAPTER ONE

The last crow of the cockerel signaled the final warning to those yet to finish their early morning chores. The sun was rising steady and its early morning rays could be felt by anyone outside at the moment. While the birds sang, the animals chewed on what was left of last night's dinner as they prepared for another outing in the fields. The villagers were not left out of the morning's activities. The farmers hurriedly prepared to leave for their farms, the herdsmen prepared to leave for the grazing fields before the sun sets. Indeed it was daybreak in Boma village.

Every day break meant the beginning of a new day plus a host of challenges to overcome. But this particular day was going to mark the beginning of strange events in this once peaceful village.

Just before sunrise, Udago one of the men living in the outskirts of the village had been up. As he rushed to the river for a quick dip the sight of vultures attracted him.

5

"These vultures and their desire for flesh," he said softly as he drew closer to take a look at the carcass on the ground. Animal carcass was not a new thing in Boma village, at times a cow or sheep would stroll away and fall into the river where they would drown and will be washed onto the beach. At other times a cow could be bitten by some of the poisonous snakes common in the area and would die from the venom injected into its blood by the snake.

Thus in the morning the villagers will wake up to discover one of their cows dead. Being very strong worshipers of deities, a live cow will be buried as a gift to Rorche their god. Rorche was the deity associated with protecting the people as well as their belonging, from all kinds of evil attack.

Udago pressed forward with the intention of identifying the object that had made the vultures to gather so early in the morning. The vultures were not unaware of the intruder moving closer to them.

As Udago drew closer the vultures continued to shift uncomfortably away from what they perceived as danger preparing to take flight to safety should the intruder become violent. But the sight a few meters in front of Udago stopped him dead on his tracks. Instead of the usual tail and the hind legs, Udago saw human toes and torn clothing's. He screwed his eyes and came closer to take a better look.

I'm sure my eyes are not deceiving me; it is a human being… a boy! With this reaction he ran back towards the village as fast as his legs could carry him.

This sudden action frightened the vultures badly and caused them to fly off issuing cries of protest at having been disturbed from what would have turned out to be a fantastic meal.
Shortly after Udago delivered his news, it spread like wild fire. The men of Boma village gathered fast and began moving towards the spot where the corpse was sighted by their kinsman. The group was divided in their minds some felt it was true while other members of the group believed it was a false alarm and were already thinking of a possible punishment for Udago. A punishment that

would serve as a deterrent to any other person who might want to raise a false alarm in future.

"It's a corpse indeed and a boy too," Ogadi announced on reaching the spot.

"Udago was right, it's not a false alarm," Abokito added.

Accompanied by the men, Abokito and his men came forward to examine the corpse. "The vultures have not done much damage yet," Abokito announced to the search party. "But apparently the boy has been dead for long and it is clear he had been killed" Ogadi added moving away from the corpse.

This fact was incontestable as there was a large hole on his chest.

"What is this?" Abokito asked the men with him.

"What is that? Ogadi replied moving back towards the corpse.

Ogadi was the second-in-command of the group, himself and Abokito had similar traits. Both men were good hunters and efficient herdsmen and the fruits of their hard work could be seen. Pointing to the hole on the boy's chest, Abokito turned to look at Ogadi. "What kind of animal may have done this?" Abokito wondered loud.

"I don't know but there are many wild animals in this area," Ogadi answered scanning the area as if the killer was hiding somewhere around.

Abokito was not convinced. "It's not an animal this is the work of a man," he blurted out.

"Are you sure?" Ogadi asked "let us not raise an alarm yet, it's too early for that" he cautioned.

Looking around "where is Udago?" Abokito asked.

"I am here," Udago said stepping forward. At this point the other men now fully convinced were pressing forward to see whose son the boy was.

"Udago, I want you to tell us everything that you know about this dead boy" Ogadi demanded having received the mandate of his leader to do so.

Clearing his voice, Udago once again began narrating how he had come out and was on his way to the river when he saw the vultures.

"…On seeing the vultures I was curious" he said, "I came closer only to discover it was a human corpse and then I ran to the village to notify you all" Udago concluded.

Nodding his head in reaction to Udago's story, Abokito turned to the men.

"You and you there," Abokito said pointing at Jumba and Mumba.

"I want you to go to the village and tell the chief that his attention is urgently needed," Abokito paused and waited for Jumba and Mumba to take their exit.

"Well men of Boma village as you can see the dead boy is Halima Atanda's son, the widow whose husband died twelve months ago" Abokito informed the men.

Some of the men shook their heads in pity muttering incantations invoking the gods to protect the whole village from such gruesome murders in future.

"But who really killed this boy?" One of the men whose name was Toma asked,

"It's an animal that killed him," one of the men replied.

"Animal indeed," Toma sneered.

"Then that animal must be very skilful with a knife as to carve such a hole on his chest" Toma said sarcastically.

Ogadi smiled and nodded his head like a redneck lizard while drawing hard on his pipe. "This kind of brutal killing has never been witnessed before" Ogadi said exhaling smoke, "we must find out how and what happened here and also put a stop to it, tomorrow it could be another villager's child or even wife' Ogadi warned.

"May the gods forbid that it should happen again," Toma prayed.

Tikayo arrived the scene of the killing like a windstorm flanked by the chief priest and Mumba, Jumba brought up the rear. The chief was about asking a question but the wailing of women as Halima and some women sympathizers from the village who had also arrived to take a last look at her son interrupted him. The sight was too much for her to take she passed out but was immediately revived. Two tragedies in such a short time was a great abomination.

"That is not my son" Halima said on opening her eyes "my son is not dead, he will return to the house when he has finished playing with his mates... Atandaa..a..a where're you?" She screamed.

"Take her away" Abokito said to the women. Halima refused to budge.

"Why should I go and leave my son, I must take Uriji with me... can't you see he's all that I have?" Halima asked. Then she burst into another round of wailing. This time the women succeeded in leading her away. In Boma village women were not allowed to touch dead bodies not to mention participating in the actual burial. It was a taboo and any woman who violated this order would have her hair shaved and would be isolated for three months.

While the wailing lasted Tikayo watched without interest and as soon as Halima was taken away.Tikayo cleared his voice and began to speak.

"Men of Boma village something terrible has happened to us," he began. "May Rorche never allow it again".

"ashe" the men chorused in answer to his prayer.

"Maybe the gods are angry" the chief priest chipped in.

"Then we must offer a sacrifice to Rorche for protection," Tikayo suggested. "Any way I'll advice that you all watch over your families like the mother hen protecting her chicks" he advised.

"I know we shall catch the killer sooner or later," Ogadi said.

A burial team was raised on the spot and equipped with digging implements the four man team moved towards the burial spot to commence digging. It was a taboo to keep the body of any one who died mysteriously for a long time.

"Men we must be careful with this corpse and let's hurry the burial so that the evil spirits hovering over the corpse will go away" Abokito said.

When the digging of the grave was completed the body was wrapped in a mat and the men walked round it three times each, smacking their chest each time.

Then Ogadi with the permission of the chief priest stepped forward stopping a few inches from the corpse.

"Uriji son of the late Atanda twelve months ago your father died and was buried. Today you too have embarked on this journey to another land," he paused for a while "we'll miss you even as you've left us so early we know that something or somebody has caused you to go on this journey and as we bury you we hope that as you unite with your father… the great hunter together you'll hunt down the killer so that he does not kill more. We pray you and your father to watch over us who remain and with Rorche's protection may this never happen again"Ogadi concluded.

As Uriji's corpse was lowered into the ground, the men stamped their feet and clapped their hands until the last earth was dropped.

CHAPTER TWO

The Wangoo River is one of the longest rivers in Africa and was discovered a long time ago by the inhabitants of Waroko village. Wangoo River flows through many villages before entering Zamba village from where it moves on and on. Nobody in the village knows where it ends, the Wangoo River is rich in fishes and it serves the various communities in many other ways such as providing them with a good source of water supply for all their needs. Then after the rains as the flood water recedes leaving behind a rich layer of silt which helps to enrich the top soil thus paving the way for a good farming season.

The Boma people are not found near the riverbanks like other villages. They dwell in the rich plains of the Wangoo river valley where there is green grass in abundance for their teeming herds of cattle. But the Wangoo plans are also infested with tse tse flies and mosquitoes. Compared to the lush green grass these pests are of little or no problems at all to the Boma people.

Boma village is uniquely positioned by nature. To the north, is the Wangoo river while to the south are the rolling plains of green grass better known as the Wangoo river Valley to the east and west is a thick forest rich with all that makes a forest but to the average Boma man you're looking at the evil forest. As a result of the people's perception nobody farms there, rather it is seen as a place of punishment for doers of evil. If a man is guilty of sleeping with another man's wife he is banished into the forest for five moons but if the man is guilty of killing another man he could be killed too by hanging or by being banished into the forest it all depends on the decision of the chief priest and the people of Boma village.

Where the punishment for murder is banishment, the murderer is taken to the evil forest and left there to live out his wretched life till he dies and is eaten by wild animals. If during the course of his banishment he is found near the village, he will be arrested, bound and taken back to the evil forest. Thus, the people of Boma village always avoided committing heinous crimes because the punishment is better imagined than served. Banishment into the evil forest meant certain death the average Boma man is not a coward but he would rather die for a worthy cause like protecting his territory from any aggressor than be banished into the evil forest for adultery or murder and there to die without a proper burial.

Occupation wise Boma people are cattle rearers and their cattle dot the Wangoo river valley. Unlike the Fulani herdsmen who move from place to place the Boma cattle rearers lead a sedentary life taking out their cow in the morning to the valley where the cow eat grass to their satisfaction and in the evening they lead them back to the village.

Boma women are mostly subsistence farmers growing crops and staple foodstuffs, which they sometimes trade with other villages for their own needs. The Wangoo river valley supports their lifestyle in that the grass remains green for the good part of the year and when the dry season arrives they provide the cattle with other alternatives available.

This could range from allowing them graze around the perimeter of the evil forest to feeding on anything edible within the fringes of the village. Due to their way of life Boma people have remained where they are for a very long time and it is obvious that they are there to stay.

The people of Boma village are known for their peaceful and quiet disposition but when provoked they always rise to the occasion. But so far they have been enjoying peace and prosperity with the neighboring villages. Except for skirmishes with slave merchants who attempted to enslave this people a very long time ago there has been peace. But peace and joy as the saying goes has a slender body which does not last forever the mysterious death of Uriji Atanda's son marked the beginning of problems for the villagers. Until the killer is unmasked and punished life would never be the same again for the people of

Boma village every man and woman knew that very well.

CHAPTER THREE

Kolumba Tikayo was the seventh chief of Boma village. He had been picked among the six contestants to succeed Omari Kondo the sixth chief of Boma village who had gone to join his ancestors. Picking a successor to a dead chief in Boma village was based on two criteria. At the time the chief dies, the man with the largest herd of cattle plus the biggest farm was picked as successor to the late ruler. This was significant to the people of Boma village because they believed that the chief being father of all must be able to cater for his family adequately as well as provide for any helpless villager from his reserves. After the death of chief Kondo, Tikayo was found to own the largest herds of cattle as well as the biggest farm in the land. Thus he was made the seventh chief of Boma village. Men from time in Boma village are chronic polygamists and Tikayo was no exception. The new chief of Boma village had two wives Mako and Akko with eleven children to make the family complete. Tikayo's compound was the largest in the village. But this morning Tikayo was not a happy man. He had brought his cattle for their morning ration of grass but his mind was not at rest. Many things were happening in the village and he was at the center of it all. Though the villagers did not know yet, but for how long would it last he wondered. Leaving the cows to fend for themselves, Tikayo moved away a bit and went on to sit on a big log of wood where he once again did a flip to the past. Boma village had been in existence for many years; he was born and bred on the exact spot where the village currently stood.

He had grown into boyhood then into manhood taking on big challenges and overcoming them like when he killed a big lion that was troubling the village. Within that period he had gotten married to his wife.. Mako while Akko his second wife had followed shortly after and since then he had sired eleven children. The responsibilities were enormous but he had shown that he was equal to the task and worthy to be the next chief of Boma village. While his family grew in leaps and bounds, Boma village prospered too. There had been good harvest in the farms and the animals, especially the cows had increased tremendously in the past years.

The chicken and the goats were not left out either; all had grown in large numbers. But above all the people had known peace and happiness. There had been deaths in the village, but this had not deemed the fact that Boma village was indeed favoured by the gods. Growing up Tikayo had watched chiefs succeed each other, things had not changed rather the people of Boma village continued to prosper. But suddenly ten years after his ascension as chief of Boma village the slender body of joy was suddenly beginning to break and he was at a loss over what to do to arrest the situation. If the problem had been from one of his subjects he would have dealt with it. Had it been a case of aggression from the surrounding villages he would have decisively dealt with it and closed the chapter long ago. But the problem was not from his subjects neither was it a case of aggression from the surrounding villages. The problem was within him…in short he was the problem plaguing his domain and there was nobody to save him and neither could he save himself.

The incident, which had so dramatically altered his life overnight and was gradually pushing him to self-destruction, had occurred not too long ago. He had taken his cattle to the valley for grazing all had gone well so far. The cows had had their fill of the juicy grass, and as the sun began to go down. Tikayo had rounded up his cows and the journey home had begun. They had not covered up to ten yards when he sighted a big bird that looked like an eagle, wedged under its claws was a medium sized object, which he could not identify immediately. Just then the bird came under attack from its aerial neighbors, in a bid to fight back, defend itself as well as its dinner the object dropped and landed on the ground with a slight thud.

'What could this bird be carrying?' he wondered. With the question in mind, Tikayo raced towards the object while the bird flew on making lots of funny sounds probably its own way of protesting the loss of its dinner.

On reaching the spot Tikayo bent down to examine the object but it was not necessary as he soon discovered it was flesh and still fresh". Where could this bird have gotten this? He wondered. The bird may have picked it from the carcass of an animal probably killed by a lion or some other stronger predator. Well it was his luck at least this would mean more meat in his soup bowl. Picking up the piece of flesh, which he discovered was a liver of an animal he returned to his herd of cattle and the journey home continued.

Reaching home, Tikayo sank his bulky frame into his favorite seat. His intention was to rest for a while before going to take a wash.

"Mako" he called "Makooo" he called a second time. This time his children heard him clearly one of them ran into the inner yard to fetch Mako. While Tikayo reclined his back on his chair and continued mulling over the day's activities. His thoughts were interrupted when Mako tapped him lightly on the knee to announce her presence.

"Welcome, my master," she greeted kneeling. Tikayo grunted a response just as he picked up the package and gave to her.

"Its liver," she said on opening it.

"Of course what else did you think it was?" Tikayo fired back.

"Master where did you get this liver?" she asked. Tikayo pretended not to hear

"My master did you go hunting today?" Mako persisted. Tikayo looked her over from head to toe and that was it as she fled towards the kitchen.

"Foolish woman," Tikayo remarked while wondering why she did not wait for him to answer, as it would have turned out to be an evening she would wish to forget in a hurry. Instead of rushing to prepare his evening meal she rather wanted to know first where the meat came from. He cursed her some more asking the gods to visit her in their fiery displeasure. Mako was Tikayo's first wife, more like the wife of his youth. Mako was given out in marriage to Tikayo due to the latter's bravery as a hunter and for being among the few in Boma village to kill a lion at an early age. Mako's father was a village elder and a big farmer. Finally his evening meal was served by Mako his first wife and assisted by two of her children. After laying the dishes the children withdrew while his wife sat opposite him so as to answer to any queries that may arise from the cooking.

"Ehm," Tikayo began "let me warn you, the next time you question me again in this house you're finished."

"Sorry my master, it won't happen again," his wife apologized.

"By the way I hope all the liver is here?" Tikayo inquired indicating his soup plate.

"Yes! My master it is all in your plate" Mako answered.

"Are you sure, tell me the truth so that the gods do not strike you down," Tikayo warned.

"The spirit of my dead father forbids that I should lie to my master in this matter," Mako replied. Thus the questioning ceased as her husband continued with his meal-pushing piece after piece of liver and meat into his mouth. With the last morsel of food in his mouth, Tikayo picked his water jug took a deep drought before setting it down. Pushing away the tray that had contained his evening meal, he gave a loud belched and watched with lack of interest as Mako cleared the dishes. Later while resting on his favourite chair, Tikayo could not help but bring back memories of the taste of the liver in his mouth.

"This liver was really delicious I've never eaten anything like this before in my life". He muttered quietly. 'I wonder which type of animal owns this delicious liver..' Tikayo dozed off still sitting on his chair and so began his problems and the urge to satisfy it.

The next day before going out with his cattle, Tikayo called Akko his second wife. "kill that big he-goat today and prepare the liver for me" he instructed.

"Yes my master" Akko answered.

But that evening Tikayo was disappointed "rubbish," he said, "this is nothing compared to the liver that I ate the previous day". He calmed down and continued with his meal; maybe tomorrow some thing else maybe a big cockerel will be killed maybe that will be the answer to his search. The next day, the third crowing of the cockerel found Tikayo ready to move out with his cattle.

"Mako," he called.

"Yes my master," she answered running towards him.

"It is your turn to cook for me today so; I want that big cockerel killed and the heart and liver preserved for me. Do you hear?" He asked.

"yes my master," Mako answered.

"In case you don't know I'm referring to that one," he said pointing at a big black cockerel.

"My master I've seen it, I will prepare your meal the way you like it." Mako assured him. Satisfied Tikayo left for the grazing fields.

Again Tikayo was disappointed the liver was not worth eating at all. Where did this mysterious liver come from? he wondered . Anyway! He told himself I shall find out if it means entering the evil forest itself I shall do just that provided I find the animal that has this tasteful liver and when I find it I shall pass a law making it an offence for anybody that kills this particular animal to eat its liver.

The liver was to be taken to the chief only he concluded quietly. Five weeks later Tikayo was still searching for the mysterious liver and he made sure it remained unknown to the villagers.

Animals upon animals were slaughtered yet none of their livers matched the mysterious liver. On his part Tikayo was far from ready to give up his desire to locate the source of this liver. He yearned for that blissful moment with the delicious liver being crushed to bits by his powerful set of teeth with his stomach as final destination.

The search for the animal with the special liver continued until almost every possibility was exhausted within the village. Then he turned his attention to all the forest around Boma village including the evil forest. He hunted down many animals but in the end he was totally disappointed and he itched terribly for a taste of liver... his favourite liver.

Tikayo eventually became frustrated due to his inability to get another liver as delicious as the one he had eaten earlier on. Desperation set in and it became a real obsession whereby the Boma chief would rage at the slightest provocation. His family was the worst for it and he no longer enjoyed his meals. Knowing well that he had not sampled all the animals in the forest Tikayo decided to embark on a bizarre decision that was to change the life of Boma people, for as long as it would last.

At the back of his mind was a nagging feeling that the liver could be human liver but how can I kill my subject or somebody in my house just to get his liver? He wondered. But I must have this liver again; he said to himself Tikayo weighed the prospect carefully but the delicious feeling of the first liver in his mouth was too much for him to bear. I can't take this punishment anymore I must have this liver. The urge could not be ignored anymore it must be satisfied.

With his mind made up on the issue he had laid an ambush along one of the old farm route, which had been partly discarded. He had waited patiently for his victim irrespective of whether it turned out to be his own child.

Unfortunately, the first victim turned out to be Atanda's son and he had paid the price. It had been easy killing the boy Tikayo had combined surprise, strength and speed to overcome his victim.

Three heavy blows to the head and the boy had gone down without a sound. Elated Tikayo then brought out his hunting knife and quickly made a path to his vital organ where he cut out the liver he then dragged the corpse to the spot where it was later discovered. Then Tikayo after cleaning himself of bloodstain had proceeded home. That evening he was his old self again as he munched on the liver of one of his subjects he was obsessed and he knew it but he did not care.

Tikayo had enjoyed his meal tremendously and the boy's corpse had been found by Udago and it had been buried after undergoing an impromptu funeral rite and that had been it. Nobody was suspecting him after all nobody had caught him in the act. That was then but during his sober moment he shuddered at his actions. How was he going to get out of this mess without hurting himself first and his family he wondered?

He fantasized with a couple of options that included killing himself but he rejected the idea. Why should he kill himself he wondered? As far as he was concerned that was a cowardly way out. In every society there are people who must be sacrificed for the society to survive. People must die for society to survive and Boma village was not an exception by a long shot therefore suicide was out of the question he will not do it so that his body will not be thrown into the evil forest. A thief is only declared a thief when he is caught in the act of stealing or with the stolen item. Life was sweet and he would continue as if nothing had ever happened. From henceforth I must be careful in the manner with which I source for my liver. He cautioned himself. Tikayo also resolved that after killing his victim and removing the liver rather than leave the body where it will be found thereby drawing undue attention and unnecessary talk he would hide the body first then in the night when the entire village was asleep he would come out and bury the body in the bush. The villagers would search and make plenty noise about the missing person and extensive sacrifices would be made to rorche for protection and for the safe return of the missing person. But how far Tikayo would go in his killing only time was the best judge.

The killing or rather the mysterious death of Atanda's son passed faster than anybody in Boma village anticipated. For the moment peace returned to Boma village again. From a casual observation of the village it was obvious that life had returned to normal. Two things attested to this fact the first being that the women could afford to leave for their farms alone unaccompanied by their husbands.

The second fact was the children who also enjoyed the liberty of running about like little antelopes just released from cages. Moreover unlike in the past, the children could now afford to go to the river in their different groups to enjoy themselves. The average father or mother in Boma village is never afraid that his child might drown. This confidence is attributed to the fact that in

Boma village, the moment a child comes out of her mother's womb after the separation of the umbilical chord the child is taken to the river for a brief welcome ceremony into the world. Even though they lived some distance away from the river the forefathers of the village still thought it wise that every Boma child be brought up in this way with this initiation done the river becomes a friend of the child and no discouragement is entertained from the mother.

The child continues in this manner and by the time the child is six years old the child would have mastered the first basic steps of swimming and the fear of large bodies of water is already removed. Beyond this the children are trained to hunt for animals like their fathers.

Thus, the mothers were not afraid when their children venture to the river. Having the confidence that the children were already equipped to face life. The mothers watched with joy as their children pranced about, as far as they were concerned whatever had held the village to ransom had gone and their children could once again enjoy themselves to their hearts content.

While the people of Boma village went about their daily activities, without the fear of death resulting from attacks by the phantom that had laid siege on the village. The same could not be said of Tikayo the chief of Boma village. Tikayo was a worried man, but he was always careful so as not to give himself away but whenever he was alone, Tikayo always cursed everything that had contributed to his problems.

That Tikayo was not afraid was a joke. Unless he found an alternative to the human liver, he would go on killing and one day he would be caught and that would mean being banished to the evil forest to die a wretched death or be hanged.

"Curse be the day I set my eyes on that mysterious liver," Tikayo said smacking a nearby tree with his right palm. This action drew a grunt from his cattle grazing a couple of feet away from him. "Now what do I do? He asked himself "How do I get out of this problem?"

Tikayo continued to ponder on the issue at hand turning it over and over in his mind; he continued to weigh the option that had just entered his mind. This pleased him a lot and he smiled in total relief. As far his predicament was concerned, this might just be the final solution to his nightmare. May be the antelope might have this liver too if it does then he won't be killing human beings again.

Leaving his herd of cattle to graze on its own. Tikayo left and began walking into the forest in search of the antelope. So far, after killing the Atanda boy, Tikayo had been experimenting by killing other animals so far he was not satisfied. He believed the antelope had a liver similar to that of a human being. He had slaughtered a couple of his cows but he did not get what he wanted too.

He had resorted to hunting animals like rabbits; grass cutters etc. Heavily disappointed especially with the grass cutters, Tikayo had finally resolved to go for the bigger game. As he trudged along the path, Tikayo could not help salivating as his mind went back to the last liver he had had. As far as he was concerned, it was ages since he had a decent meal spiced with his favourite liver.

Suddenly, a grass cutter darted across his path. He let it go, for that was not the kind of game he was after. To ensure that he was not caught off guard, Tikayo picked an arrow from his pouch and placed it on his bow. He was a very good hunter and everybody in his village knew it and it was not a secret that the Family he descended from had been good hunters too and successful cattle owners. Enough of this family history, he would think about it some other time but for now he was badly in need of a good meal spiced with his delicious liver.

Suddenly he saw the footmarks of an average sized animal he examined them "antelope," he said. Rising up immediately he became very alert and started following the tracks on the soft earth. Tikayo continued tracking the animal but did not see it. On the verge of giving up, he heard the sound of chewing carefully, Tikayo quietly crawled towards the sound on sighting his target Tikayo heaved a sigh of relief. Standing a few meters from him was a big brown antelope that was busy feeding unaware of the danger before it.

With his arrow fixed to the bow, Tikayo stealthily closed the distance between himself and the antelope. Deftly he released the arrow straight into the thigh of the animal incapacitating it in the process. The antelope let out a whine and slumped to the ground. Tikayo immediately rushed towards the antelope with all the speed he could muster. He brought out a very sharp hunting knife and without delay slashed the throat of the animal as the blood flowed, Tikayo collected the amount he could in a medium sized gourd. He then opened up the antelope; he did not probe too long before finding the liver. "Wooo" he exhaled. The much-coveted prize was now within reach; first he cut out the bile and threw it away.

As a boy his father had told him, "Animals are crafty". Not knowing what that meant he had probed further, "good" his father had said "As a hunter the moment you bring down an animal whether in a group or alone, the first thing to do is to open it up and cut out the bile. If you delay, you will not like the taste later".

"What is the reason for that?" Tikayo asked.

"Like I said before most animals are crafty in that at the throes of death, most animals secrete lot of bile which makes its flesh bitter therefore when you strike immediately slash the throat if it is still alive and then dissect it and cut off the bile. Do this and the flesh remains fit for consumption."

Truly Tikayo had experimented and he had seen the truth in what his father had said. Throughout his transition from boyhood to manhood, he had always remembered this advice.

Thus with all manner of love he severed the bile sac from the animal's organs, and then he cut off the liver and carefully dropped it into his bag. "Now I will gather the carcass of the antelope and drag it home. Thanks to Rorche there would be meat in abundance for my entire wives and children".

CHAPTER FOUR

Tikayo reached his compound just before sunset. Throwing down his load he sank his frame into his favourite chair and tried to relax as his children rushed out of their abodes to greet him.

"Have you children had your evening food?" He asked.

"Yes," Okanu answered on behalf of the other children. Okanu was the second son of the entire family. Tall for his age, Okanu was a tough lad and like his elder brother he was showing signs of growing up into a strong lad and a good hunter.

"Where is your mother?" Tikayo asked Komo another child of his.

"In the kitchen," Komo answered.

"Call her for me now," he ordered.

"Yes papa," Komo replied racing off to fetch his mother. Tikayo continued relaxing and mulling over the day's activities.

"Yes my master here am I," his second wife said tapping him gently on the knee.

"Whose turn is it to cook today?" he asked.

"It's my turn," she replied.

"Is my food ready? Tikayo asked

"Yes, my master" she said rising up to go.

"Wait," he said. Dipping his hand into the bag he produced a medium sized bundle.

"Akko you know I love the liver of animals very much?" he asked.

"Today it's your turn to cook my favourite for me.. do it well."

"I'll do my best my Lord," Akko promised and went back into the kitchen.

Akko was the second wife of Tikayo chief of Boma village she had been married to him for many years and she had borne him six beautiful strong children. As soon as his second wife vanished from view, Tikayo reclined back on the chair and closed his eyes while allowing his mind to go on a roller coaster. He dwelt extensively on the predicament facing him. He had killed many animals in the past months and had eaten their liver; it was not to be compared with that first liver he had eaten previously. He had killed two people in Boma village already and it was clear that the liver he had eaten before was human liver.

He did not like killing innocent villagers besides two deaths in a short space of time. The entire village was now on alert but that did not pose a problem to a skilled hunter like himself "No matter how alert they maybe I shall still get my meat. I pray that this antelope liver will turn out to be a good substitute, he mumbled to himself.

"My master what are you substituting?" A voice asked suddenly from behind. Tikayo was badly frightened and he showed it.

"How many times have I warned you not to take me unaware again?" He asked his wife with eyes blazing. Akko carrying a tray laden with a big bowl of fufu and okro soup rich with the antelope liver halted immediately and she remained rooted on the spot to take in the rebuke. Remaining on the spot like a statue, Akko stayed in that position till she was sure that her husband's anger had abated.

"I am sorry my master," Akko said by way of apology as she kneeled to serve him his evening meal.

"I've heard you," he said gruffly. "Make sure you don't do that again else you will be sorry for yourself."

"Yes my master I shall remember your warning," Akko pledged. With the matter rested, Tikayo began to attack the big bowl of fufu before him. He isolated the liver in his soup bowl preferring to tackle it last.

"I hope this is the liver that I gave you to prepare?" Tikayo asked.

"Yes my master it is the liver that you gave me to prepare," Akko replied. There was silence as he ate on, suddenly he fired another question

"What kind of liver is this?" he asked taking a second bite to be very sure. Akko was confused but remained silent.

Tikayo was disappointed his experiment didn't work. I shall kill again, he vowed silently. Tikayo and his wife maintained the silence as he continued eating. As the chief of Boma village, Tikayo ran his house with utmost ruthlessness. It was a taboo to talk while he was eating. You had to also suspend all that you were doing to listen and you must stand till he had finished speaking. His wives and children had more than a healthy respect for him. He was like a god to his family and in the entire village he was highly respected for his strength and prowess as a hunter. Tikayo was the third man among the hunters in Boma village to kill two lions and follow it with a tiger using just his bow and arrow in both cases.

"Water," he suddenly called out. Akko as alert as ever reached out and served him drinking water in a big jug.

Tikayo then reclined his back on his rocking chair followed with a subdued belch. He watched with disgust as Akko and her children cleared the partly empty dishes of what had earlier been his dinner. He had not enjoyed the meal at all especially the liver, which was that of an antelope. "Only the human liver taste so delicious and I shall continue to kill to satisfy my urge. Henceforth I must enjoy my meals! On the spot Tikayo silently resolved to have a good meal as from the following day.

Tikayo lived up to his promise as he returned from the field with a package the following day. It was Mako's turn to cook remembering the first warning she did not ask questions. That evening Tikayo ate well emptying his plate. A feat he had not achieved for a long time. This time he followed it with a loud belch, which could be heard by those around him. As the plates were being taken away he patted, his stomach here lies the liver of my third victim. The liver he had eaten that evening was that of a twelve-year-old boy from Boma village.

In his quest to satisfy his urge Tikayo was very careful to limit his attacks to only children and women from Boma village. The other neigbouring villages he knew would not take the disappearance of their kinsman kindly. Knowing well the kind of powers these villages had Tikayo decided to play soft by not killing somebody who was not from Boma village. As chief of Boma village Tikayo at a glance could tell his subjects from other villagers. One feature that gave them away was the marks on their faces and their pierced ears, which always had an earring dangling. It was not because Boma village was scared of fighting after all they were warriors. But Tikayo thought it foolish to provoke war through his actions. So he thus limited himself to Boma village.

CHAPTER FIVE

Despite the red alert in the village, it was still easy to bag a lonely victim. After all the mothers still sent their children sometimes alone on errands to the farm or villages to get an item for the house.

Tikayo was standing on the slope watching his herd of cattle, feeding when he saw the boy pass on his way to a nearby village to acquire some items.

"There goes my next victim," he'd said to himself. Immediately he went into action, by laying a trap the type he used to catch animals in Boma forest. With the trap laid Tikayo hid in the nearby bush and waited the return of the boy. Armed with a dull object, he patiently awaited the return of his would be victim.

For a while he feared his victim had taken another route back to the village. Disappointed, he was about coming out to dismantle the trap when he heard the faint sound of singing in the distance, immediately he rushed back into hiding. Presently, the boy reached the spot where the trap was buried. A piece of metal from the trap was sticking out rather than move on the boy stopped and came closer to investigate. Probing with his toe the big trap sprang free and caught his right foot. "A trap," he muttered very amused at the stupidity of his peers to bury a trap in such a place. He would laugh at them and teach them how to lay traps in the right places. First, he must get the trap off his feet. He was so engrossed with the attempts to free his right foot; he never knew what happened and will never know. For like a curious cat, he had paid the price for his curiosity.

All the while that the boy played with the trap, Tikayo was calmly watching. The moment it caught his foot Tikayo prepared to pounce. As the boy was trying to get his right foot out of the trap, Tikayo came quietly behind him and dealt him two powerful blows on the head with his club and the boy died without a sound. Gazing at the corpse it dawned on him that he had just snuffed out another life.

"I've killed again," he said quietly to himself. Then realizing that he was standing on the path that was frequently used by the villagers he quickly dragged the corpse into the bush he had used to lay in wait for his victim. Dissecting his victim was not a difficult task because he was always prepared for such situations. He brought out the heart and the liver from the warm body and carefully wrapped it with leaves, smiling as he dropped it into his hunting bag. After covering the boy with leaves, Tikayo then washed his hands carefully with the water he carried in his herdsman's calabash and then he returned to round up his cattle to take them home for the day.

Shortly after turning in for the night, the Boma chief discovered he could not sleep. Lying alone in his bed in his hut, Tikayo was racked by thoughts on the crime he was committing, killing the future generation of Boma village to satisfy a deadly desire. He was hooked on human liver like a man gets hooked to booze and women. How do I break out of this habit, he wondered as he tossed from one side of the bed to the other. Matters were made worse by the fact that none of his wives was sleeping with him tonight maybe after a moment of passion with any of his wives he would have been able to get a good night's rest. Tikayo continued tossing from one side of the bed to the other trying to drive away the ghosts that were hunting him. Eventually a few hours before dawn, Tikayo drifted into an uneasy sleep filled with bad dreams.

At the second crow of the cockerel, Tikayo was fully awake and seated on his wooden bed with his head buried in his two hands. He had not slept well at all last night and just as he was hoping to make the best of the opportunity left the cockerels began to crow signalling the beginning of another day. Tikayo was still trying to come to terms with the bad dreams of the previous night when he heard a light knock on the door. He ignored the knocking initially believing that whoever it was will go away after a while. But when the knocking persisted he got up and went on to answer.

"Who is it?" he asked opening the door in the process.

"Good morning father," his son Okanu greeted.

"What do you want that I must be disturbed so early in the morning?" Tikayo queried brushing aside his son's greetings. Okanu informed his father that a woman from the village wanted to see him.

"What does she want?" Tikayo asked, a deep frown creasing his face.

"Father, I do not know," Okanu replied. "Okay go on I shall be there soon," he said.

"Yes father." Okanu answered walking away.

I wonder what this woman wants from me, Tikayo reflected as he went into the yard.

"Good morning my master," his wives chorused. Replying with a wave of the hand, he motioned the woman to come closer.

"Good morning my master and May you live long as the ruler of our village." The early morning visitor greeted.

"Thank you and if the Gods so wish," Tikayo replied. "I was told you wanted to see me?" he asked.

"Yes my master," the woman replied. With the prompting of his hand the woman began to speak.

"Yesterday just before the going down of the sun I sent Utako to the next village to…"

"Who is Utako?" Tikayo asked interrupting her.

"Sorry my master, Utako is my second child," she replied.

Nodding his head, Tikayo asked her to continue with her narration.

"…he was to get me some ingredients for my cooking but up to this moment Utako has not shown up. I am worried my Lord help me…" and she burst into tears.

"Easy, my daughter," he consoled. "Where is your husband?"

"He left home very early in the company of two friends to make enquiries at the other village." Tikayo's heart missed a beat at the news for he now knew that the liver and heart that he had for supper belonged to his subject

- a boy named Utako. Snapping out of his reverie he faced Utako's mother.

"My daughter I feel your pain in that I am a father and would be terribly upset if any evil should befall my children–may the gods not allow it," Tikayo said as he paused.

"ashe," the woman responded.

"Well my daughter you go home and let me handle this issue with the elders of the village," Tikayo promised. Utako's mother burst into a fresh round of tears as she made her exit out of the chief's compound watched by members of Tikayo's household.

"What are you looking at?" Tikayo barked at them. "Is this the first time you've seen a woman crying…?" They didn't wait for him to finish before dispersing to face their early morning chores.

"Stupid people," he cursed under his breath.

Adjusting his bulky frame on his rocking chair, Tikayo drifted into thoughts. This ugly trend must stop; within a space of five months he had snuffed out three lives to satisfy a craving for human liver. Right there on his chair, Tikayo felt as if an enormous monster was crushing him. The noose was closing gradually and he dreaded the kind of fate that would befall him if he were eventually caught. But how do I get out of this mess, he pondered quietly. May be he will go to the chief priest but he won't confess he would only say he was possessed by an evil spirit from the evil forest and thus he needed deliverance. This thought pleased him very much and he smiled in satisfaction as he got up to take his cattle out for the day.

Before leaving home for the fields, Tikayo called his village elders together for a very brief but crucial meeting.

"The agenda for this meeting is Utako's mysterious disappearance while on an errand for his mother," Tikayo said. He and the elders talked for quite a while bringing in the past killings of two other children.

"All the other villages have washed their hands clean of these atrocities," Ogadi said.

"If only we could catch the killer then this nightmare would be over". Tikayo added feigning annoyance. But for the moment it was agreed that a search party be raised to carry out a thorough search of the bushes and routes.

"It's a good idea," Toma said, "it might be that the boy just missed his way due to the naughtiness inherent with children who were bound to explore their surroundings."

"And I think we should perform a sacrifice to Rorche," Tikayo suggested. The elders with one voice agreed to their chief's suggestion. Before dispersing Tikayo told the elders to inform the chief priest on the need to perform sacrifices. "The gods must protect the people of Boma village from harm," Tikayo said strongly.

"Ashe," the men chorused together as they dispersed for the day's activities.

CHAPTER SIX

The search party constituted by Tikayo in his capacity as chief and led by a skilled hunter named Kato went into action immediately; they conducted their search independent of the search team led by Utako's father. The people of Boma village were confident that Utako would be found alive and well.

"The people are depending on us to find Utako," Kato told his team. "And we must not let them down."

"May the gods grant us speed," one of the men added. "Utako will come home alive," Jobanga said. Jobanga was the younger brother to Utako. "After all, besides the chief, father is the next best hunter in Boma village."

His mother could not help but share in his childish imagination. "Let us continue to pray and believe that the gods of our ancestors will help us in these difficult moments." Utako's mother added. Mother and son then lapsed into silence each engrossed in their different thoughts. Utako's mother after replaying the scene that had taken place the morning she went to the chief's compound to report the disappearance of Utako could not help but marvel at the way the chief had behaved.

On many occasions she had noticed that the chief while talking suddenly drifted off and thereby lost consciousness of those around him. Could it be that the chief knew something about their missing son because the distant look in his eyes that morning made him look like one with knowledge of what was happening? She shook herself out of her daydreaming, how could it be? It can't be true that the chief knew something. I had better be careful of what I say before Boma people finish me. But all the same she made a note to discuss her thoughts with her husband any time he returned from the search for their missing son. At least there was no crime in confiding in your husband. The worst that could happen would be a stern rebuke from her husband warning her not to ever allow such foolish thoughts into her head again or else she would get the beating of her life with a scar or two for future remembrance. At the moment she continued beseeching the gods that her son would be brought back to her.

Time moved fast, as the villagers began returning home her apprehension rose. Moreover the sun was going down very fast and it will soon be dark and of course no sensible person would continue searching for a missing boy under cover of darkness.

"Oh Rorche! The God of my forefathers do not desert me now" Utako's mother prayed.

Shortly, the village search team arrived.

"No news of Utako," their leader said. They had searched everywhere possible without any trace of the boy.

"We've gone to the river even there no sign existed to show he had been near the river," Kato added.

Utako's mother finally lost hope when her husband's search team returned without any sign of their son.

"Oh my son, where are you?" she wailed. The floodgates suddenly gave way and she let go another round of wailing. The village women could not take it anymore they all joined in the wailing for Utako.

While his wife wailed at her misfortune, Abokito flanked by friends and sympathizers sat quietly huddled together in a small group.

"Where did we forget to search?" Abokito asked.

"Nowhere," they replied.

"Was he taken by a wild animal or did he drown in the river?" One of the sympathizers wondered aloud.

"If he was eaten by a wild animal at least his clothes would have been discovered," his father replied. "We've been to the nearby village where he went to buy the condiments the women reported seeing him come and go so he disappeared before reaching the village. I wonder what has befallen Boma village lately" Abokito lamented.

"I'm at a loss over this type of tragedy that has befallen us," Kato said.

Another day of intensive searching involving the entire inhabitants of Boma village was mounted again. The men and the women searched all the spots they believed children were likely to play. While the children also were not left out, they too searched all their hideouts in case Utako had fallen down while playing alone and was unconscious but they all came away empty handed. For good measure another rigorous search was carried out the following day involving the entire village yet Utako was not found. At this point his entire family and his playmates all gave up any hope of finding Utako again. Utako's mother was the worst hit as she wailed uncontrollably. Using all kinds of names to plead with her son to come home.

Dejectedly, they all trooped back to the village with the hope that the gods would do something never seen nor known to any mortal being. While the women and children returned home, the men made their way silently like robots to the village square where they would hold a meeting with the chief to prepare a sacrifice for the gods.

Tikayo appeared while the men were still talking in little groups of two's and three's. Flanked by the chief priest and his assistant, Tikayo moved to his usual position to take his seat while the men cut short their discussion and turned their attention on their village chief.

"Men of Boma village I greet you all," he began. The men responded in return.

"A lot have happened in this once peaceful village…" Tikayo said.

"True talk," Ogadi butted in.

"Our children are disappearing without being found. In other cases some are killed mysteriously without any trace of the killer and their bodies are mutilated with vital body parts missing." At this juncture Tikayo paused to let what he had said so far to sink in. "Now we have a big problem on our hands. It was only three days ago that I was awoken from my sleep only to come out and be told that a child had mysteriously disappeared without any trace while on errand for his mother. The boy as it were turned out to be Utako the son of Abokito one of our great hunter and herdsman. By the way where is my good friend Abokito?" Tikayo asked.

"I am here," Abokito said raising his hand from where he sat surrounded by five friends.

"I am sorry over your son and the inability of the search teams in finding him," Tikayo said by way of consolation.

"Thank you chief for your concern," Abokito said.

"These indeed are hard times for Boma village and my family. We've searched everywhere but Utako is now here to be found..." Tikayo said.

"What about the surrounding villages anything from them?" The chief priest asked.

"Nothing," Abokito said shaking his head. "...But from the village next to ours it was said that they saw Utako come in and they also saw him leave. I personally spoke with the woman he bought the condiments from and she attested to this fact."

While the narration continued by Abokito the Boma village chief was nervous over the fact that a careless mistake on his part could give him away as the culprit so it would be better if Abokito was made to stop soon.

"We've searched all the nooks and corners to no avail, right now we don't know what else to do..." Abokito added.

"Alright Abokito I feel your pain," Tikayo said interrupting him from continuing. Actually, this was the opportunity he had eagerly waited for. It was safer that he direct proceedings lest any of the men be overtaken by an evil thought and ventures on to suggest something that could land him in trouble.

"Okay men of Boma village we're all aware of what has been happening to our once peaceful village," Tikayo said, "may the gods of our forefathers restore peace in our land again,"

"ashe-ee," the men chorused.

"But we must do something to arrest this sad development," Abokito said pausing for a while. They all knew he had more to say and Tikayo listened keenly to hear the next sentence and also watched out for a way to take over proceedings again. "Men of Boma village, we are in perilous times." Abokitito announced as if the men didn't know.

"m-mm," the men chorused in answer.

"What is life if our children cannot play in their favorite places?" Abokito asked pausing again while the men listened with bated breath. The chief priest raised his face to look at the sky while Tikayo readjusted himself on his seat all the while wishing that Abokito would go on to say his piece and then shut up his big mouth.

"Men of Boma village," Abokito began demonstrating as he spoke. "what is life if our wives cannot send our children on errand anymore? I've never witnessed all these before," he said gesturing with his hands as he spoke. "Men of Boma village let's all stand up and expel the evil that has entered Boma village so that we can return to our normal lives once more, thank you."

Abokito's speech was applauded by all the men in the meeting ground

"Abokito my friend you've spoken well. I yearn for things to be normal again is there any man here that is enjoying what we're going through?" Tikayo asked.

"No-o-o-o-o," the men chorused in return.

"you see?." Tikayo continued. "We all want to return to our normal lives, we want our children to be play freely, run errands for their mothers without fear. Is that not so?"

"Yes that's what we want," the men of Boma village replied disjointedly.

"Good! As your chief I would be failing in my duty if I sit back and watch our children disappear or die mysteriously and did nothing. After all I have children of my own too so it could be my turn…"

"May our ancestors forbid that," the chief priest cut in.

"Ashe," Tikayo said. Looking around him. "That's why I summoned this meeting an evil, spirit has descended on Boma village and is attacking the very foundation and the future of Boma village by killing our children… that's why I've brought the chief priest of the village to tell us what we shall do to expel this evil spirit from our village". Tikayo took his seat amidst murmuring and grunting from the men.

"That's what I've been itching to hear all this while," Okuja said. Okuja was a herdsman too but most times he liked to hunt while his son tended the cattle. As could be seen the men of Boma village could not hide their relief over the fact that at last a far reaching solution was on the way. There was no doubt that after the sacrifice was performed the evil spirit that was attacking Boma will not go away.

"Men of Boma village I greet you all," the chief priest began, "may our ancestors continue to guide and preserve us all from every evil spirit"-

"Asheeee," the men responded.

"Our chief has told me to perform sacrifices to appease the gods so that they will drive away the evil spirit that is taking our children," the chief priest at this juncture paused for a while. "The gods have been neglected; the gods of Boma village are angry and hungry too. The people have turned their backs on the gods of their forefathers and ancestors, hence they too have turned their backs on the people of Boma village," the chief priest announced

There was murmuring among the men as they talked among themselves.

"What must we do then to appease the gods of our ancestors?" Udago asked.

"The people must beg the gods to forgive them for their foolishness and also to cleanse the land of the evil that is disturbing the people, we'll offer sacrifices to Rorche the god of land and protection so that he will protect us from evil…"

"What kind of sacrifices are we talking about?" Tikayo asked interrupting the chief priest.

"Good, at this time tomorrow we shall be resting because we would have finished the sacrifices." The Chief Priest announced.

"Very early tomorrow morning all the men of Boma village plus the chief will converge at the shrine of Rorche where the sacrifice will be done. Two cows will be used and then the men present will carry a bowl of blood each to their house and spray round their compounds and then you will dip your finger into the bowl and use it to mark the forehead of your children and wives. The meat from the carcass will be divided among the men. Nobody is to go out tomorrow." The chief priest warned.

With the conclusion by the chief priest, questions were asked and answers given. Satisfied the men rose up to go to their various homes thus ending the meeting.

Tikayo walked home with the agility of an antelope to most other men he looked like a man going to visit his newly married wife. If Tikayo was aware of all this he was not perturbed rather he was thinking of how to get his next piece of liver because the craving for that delicious piece of flesh had come on him again and he observed that he lacked the strength or will power to wish it away. Instead he would try to satisfy it. What more with the sacrifices done the people of Boma village will have the illusion that the evil spirit had left the village.

"And of course that is when I shall hit my next victim," he said to himself. Contented with his plans, he walked home just in time as his first wife was putting finishing touches to the evening meal.

"Welcome my master," she greeted and the children did the same, Tikayo merely grunted and pushing past the children he headed for his hut for a brief rest before taking his evening meal.

CHAPTER SEVEN

"All the men of Boma village, the chief request that you assemble at the shrine of Rorche" the town crier said clanging on his gong as he traversed the four corners of Boma village.

It was already time to wake up as the cockerel had crowed twice already. At the end of the meeting the previous day it had already been agreed that the sacrifice would be done this morning to appease the god of land and protection. At the third crow of the cockerel all the men of Boma village were gathered at the shrine of the gods for the "sacrifice of appeasement". Tikayo appeared, walking with the agility of a leopard made his way into the shrine to have a chat with the chief priest before commencing with the sacrifice.

On the other hand the men armed with the bowls they were to use in collecting blood were trying to make themselves comfortable when the chief priest appeared from the shrine of Rorche. Flanked by Tikayo and his assistant a fellow known as Ageri, the chief priest walked to his usual position and paused. Tikayo maintained a distance. He had dominated proceedings at the meeting; today it was the turn of the chief priest to take charge of proceedings.

Beside his title as chief priest, his real name was Roku. In the Boma dialect, Roku means fire. Roku was the fourth son of Boma village to be made chief priest in the village. His family was reputed for their fame and knowledge in spiritual matters. Three generations of his family had served as chief priest of Rorche and they had served well. Now it was the turn of Roku to continue and also uphold family tradition while at the same time attempt an appeasement with Rorche the god of Boma village so that the evil spirit that was in the land will be expelled into the forest from where it came from.

"Great and powerful Rorche the god of my ancestors I greet you…" There was silence from all the men gathered at the shrine. "Mighty and powerful Rorche the god of my Forefathers, the god of my kinsmen I greet you…" This round of greeting was followed by another moment of silence. "Great Rorche, the god of Boma village, the god that saved our forefathers from their enemies … I greet you". He then turned to face the men. "Only a mad man will go to sleep with his house on fire ehn I say only a foolish child will laugh at an old woman whereas the child will grow old one day. A child that refuses to let her mother sleep will also not sleep. Men of Boma village you've all been careless and neglected your god. That is why this evil has come upon Boma village".

The chief priest paused to let his audience absorb all that he had said so far. The silence was total such that even if a pin dropped the noise of the fallen pin would have been heard by all the people gathered at the shrine.

"Great and powerful Rorche-the god of our Forefathers…" The chief began yet another fresh round of chanting… "The god that saved our fathers from the tricks of their enemies hear us today and deliver our land from the evil that has befallen us." The chief priest went on and on with the various stages of invocation all in the bid to soften the ground before the actual killing of the cows and sprinkling of blood could commence. While it lasted, Tikayo and all the men of Boma village watched the proceedings in absolute silence. Then the chief priest entered the shrine and after a while came out as usual accompanied by his assistant.

"Men of Boma village hear me. The god of our land must be appeased, and this morning we shall slaughter these bulls," he said, pointing at the two male cows tied some couple of yards away from the shrine. Then the priest called for volunteers, immediately ten men stepped forward without delay.

"Good," the priest said. "Five men to one cow and when you cut its throat do not allow the blood to spill on the ground; rather it should be collected in a big calabash…" Immediately the men went to work, the two cows were tied up and as their throats were being slit each cow let out a loud sound before being silenced forever. The blood was collected into two calabashes and brought before the chief priest.

"Oh Rorche…." the chief priest resumed his invocation. "Your people have brought their sacrifice of appeasement receive this token from your people and deliver Boma village from the evil that, has befallen the people"

"Asheee," the men chorused. The chief priest then dipped fresh broom into the bowl of blood before him and sprinkled round the shrine. At his invitation Tikayo stepped forward and the priest dabbed his forehead with blood."

"May the gods of Boma village protect you and your household from the evil that is ravaging Boma village," the chief priest prayed.

"Ashe," Tikayo responded and moved away with his bowl containing cow blood. All the men took turns to be touched by the chief priest.

"You can now share out the meat," the chief priest ordered. The meat was shared out to all the men gathered at the shrine of Rorche that morning, with all the men prayed for the chief priest ended the proceedings.

As far as Tikayo was concerned the so-called sacrifice made to the gods was an exercise in futility. If Rorche was truly powerful let it tell the people it was him-Tikayo the chief of Boma village that was behind the killing and mysterious disappearance of the children in Boma village. That was their headache right now he was in need of a delicious piece of human flesh known as liver. It had been almost two weeks since he tasted this delicious piece of flesh but now sacrifices had been made and the people are alert so he decided to lie low.

"Yes," he said to himself. "I shall hold on for sometime and let the people believe that the sacrifice was working before striking again".

Exactly three weeks after the sacrifice was made to Rorche the god of land and protection. Tragedy struck again as Tikayo killed his next victim. It had not been difficult for him because he had attacked with the speed of a lion. His victim had fallen easily because she was not alert thus was careless about her safety. Moreover every inhabitant of Boma village except Tikayo believed the evil spirit had been expelled from Boma village and thus they could all walk about freely without let or hindrance.

How wrong they were in their assumptions, for Tikayo had only lied low for just three weeks to give them the impression that the sacrifice was successful and Rorche had finally chased away the evil spirit.

A day later Tikayo struck again, this time Tikayo made no effort to conceal the body of the woman. Why engage the people in a search in which the body might not be found? He wondered. With that in mind he carefully wrapped the liver and the heart, which he had cut from the woman's body and departed for his house. "I'm going to have a good meal once again after such a long time" he remarked to himself.

CHAPTER EIGHT

The discovery of the body had first started with an alarm being raised by the husband of the missing woman. Having come back from the grazing site Mumba had secured his herds of cattle and then walked into the yard with anticipation of his favourite meal being cooked. But a few steps into his hut he stopped like someone hit by a bolt of lightning.

"What is this?" he asked nobody. "I do not perceive the aroma of any food being cooked." Then he saw his children crying, immediately he knew something was not right.

"Come and don't cry again," Mumba said as he tried to appease his children.

"Tikko where is your mother?" he asked the eldest child.

"Mama said she was going towards the other village to see if there will be any fish to buy," the child replied. The gods be praised his wife went to arrange for soup condiments and not to gossip. He thought within him.

"Let us all be patient she'll soon be back and we shall all eat," he said in a consoling manner while patting the youngest child on the head.

Mumba then went into his hut to await the return of his wife from the market. Next time he will warn her to start the evening meal quite early. Eventually Mumba dozed off without the comfort of his evening meal. The knocking on the door made him to get up from his bed with a start. It was his eldest son Tikko.

"What is it?" Mumba said robbing his eyes. "Is your mother not yet back from the market? He asked.

"No Mama has not returned from the market," Tikko said.

"Have you eaten yet?"

"No Papa," Tikko replied.

"Where has this woman gone to?" Mumba wondered aloud. Turning to his son, "Tikko go back and search the kitchen for any left over of a previous meal". Tikko left his father and made his way to the kitchen in search of food for himself and his siblings.

Mumba sat down for a while supporting his head with both hands while his thoughts wondered on the where about of his wife. Something is terribly wrong somewhere, he told himself. It's unlike my wife to do, this he observed could the killer had come back again? Or had his wife come to some form of harm and was lying helpless on some lonely path without any form of hope or assistance? The questions continued to pour in. But sadly there was no answer to any of these questions. Rather than be contented with just sitting down to wait for his wife to stroll into their yard, Mumba got up dusted his buttocks, I'd better go and find my wife. He entered the first compound, but the response was negative from one compound he went to the other the answer was still the same... "no they had not seen his wife! Mumba was a well known figure in Boma village," was the only reply he got. Thus the news about the sudden disappearance of his wife was baffling. Initially the people of Boma village were stunned beyond belief then on recovering from the shocking news panic now descended on the entire village. Most of the men had, had supper served by their wives but at the same time they checked to make sure their children were safe. Other men whose wives after their evening food had cleared the dishes before obtaining permission to pay their friends an evening visit were quickly searched for, rounded-up and taken home by their husbands.

Boma village was under siege again as the men armed with machetes and crude spears began coming out to join Mumba in conducting a search for his missing wife. When they had reached a sizeable number they began to argue on what steps to take

"Let's divide ourselves into groups and search all the routes leading into the village," Jumba suggested.

"Three weeks ago we sacrificed to Rorche to protect us from the evil spirit that has descended on Boma village, Abokito pointed out. "Men of Boma village let us go to our chief and tell him what has happened... but I warn you, men of Boma village open your eyes and protect your families. If our gods cannot save us, maybe we should look elsewhere."

"Yes, you're right," the men murmured in agreement.

"But right now let's go to the chief," Mumba suggested.

Tikayo had finished his evening meal almost before dark and was now relaxing while his mind played back on the meal. It had been a simple meal consisting of a big bowl of fufu and groundnut soup. Unlike the last three weeks which had been a nightmare. Today's meal was memorable because it was spiced with his usual liver; he had ensured that he finished everything in his plate. His children could not hide the disappointment on their faces while clearing the dishes. The past days had been different, their father always left a lot of meat in his plate presumably for them but suddenly he had changed without warning. Tikayo was already napping on his favorite chair when one of his sons tapped him gently on the leg.

"What is it?" he asked angrily.

"The men want to see you," his son replied.

"Me? See me for what?" he asked for the umpteenth time.

"papa, I do not know," his son replied.

"Okay I shall go to them". Tikayo replied. While his son departed, Tikayo went out to meet the men of Boma village. That something was wrong was evident to him. Definitely the husband of the missing woman must be the centre of this meeting. But why think this way, he pondered. The men may have come to see him over something else.

"Men of Boma village I greet you," Tikayo said.

"We greet you too."

Without delay Mumba stepped forward to present his case. It dawned on Tikayo that the missing woman was the reason for this gathering.

"Mumba I feel for you," Tikayo said. "Right now, though it is late but we will go out still in search of Mumba's wife. No other activities are allowed tonight... but we'll meet at the village square to discuss further, when we return".

"The chief has spoken," the men said as they departed to commence the search.

At the first crow of the cockerel the next day, Mumba and the men of Boma village with the exception of their chief hit the trail again in search of Mumba's wife.

"It is obvious that a dreadful thing has happened to my wife," Mumba said to one of the men near him.

"I've told my wife never to go out alone again and to send the children in pairs to run errands," Abokito said.

"That's a good measure," Mumba said. "If we'd acted like this probably we would have known what was behind it and thus…" he never finished the statement as a shout was heard from the men searching in the opposite direction. Just then a man was seen running towards Mumba.

"Mumba come quickly and see this." With the agility of an antelope Mumba took off at top speed followed by the other men who had been searching with him. On arriving at the scene Mumba was confronted by a horrible sight he would live with for the rest of his life. On the ground lay the bloated and mutilated body of what had been his wife and the mother of his children.

"The god of my forefathers where were you when this happened?" Mumba screamed biting his teeth in exasperation. A group of men tried to lead him away from the scene. But Mumba refused to leave, "this is my wife and not some cow mistakenly shot by a hunter or killed by a wild animal," he said fighting them off.

The men of Boma village stood in clusters, completely perplexed and discussing the calamity that had be fallen their village.

"But what kind of beast is it that will kill a human being and won't eat any other part except the liver?" Abokito asked loudly just as Tikayo and the chief priest arrived to look at the body.

"Mumba's wife is dead, mutilated in this horrible manner and my son Utako mysteriously vanished into thin air, but I know I will catch the killer one day." Abokito promised.

All the men including Tikayo heard Abokito's resolve.

"My friend Abokito if you have any suggestion on how we can stop this can you please tell us all?" Tikayo requested.

Abokito laughed. "My chief how I wish I knew a way out. But I believe Rorche the god of Boma village will show me how."

A group of men were selected and together they wrapped the body of Mumba's wife to prepare it for burial.

"The body will not be taken into the village," the chief priest said. The men nodded their heads in agreement it was a custom of Boma village. Before the sun-changed direction, Mumba's wife was buried with a message that she should expose her killer and not allow them a moment's rest. Tikayo heard all the threats and prayers but he ignored them all. As far as he was concerned it was the ranting of defeated men. That was their business, he wanted a liver and he just had to get it anyhow. But right now he had business to take care of.

"Men of Boma village we'll need to sacrifice again but let us meet at the Village Square and I shall relate my reasons for this sacrifice." The Chief Priest said.

"The chief priest calling for another sacrifice," Jumba said.

"Let them do all the sacrifices and it is time Rorche told us who the killer is or else we find other means," Mumba said. Like zombies, the men of Boma village led by their chief Tikayo and the chief priest made their way back to the village. Of course the news had reached the women and the children; there was fear and uncertainty in the air. Mumba's wife had fallen victim to the madness or plague that had seized the whole of Boma village. Just like many other people that had died or disappeared without their bodies being recovered. Who would be the next victim? That seemed to be the question in the minds of the people of Boma village.

It was a moonlit night as the men of Boma village stomachs filled with their evening meal sluggishly made their way to the village square for a meeting with the village chief and the chief priest. Arriving the square most men tried to secure a comfortable place to sit, while other men tried to remove food or meat particles from their teeth. Tikayo flanked by the chief priest and his assistant walked quietly into the square and immediately the men took vantage positions so as to hear what their chief had to say. Tikayo moved into the circle created by the men.

"Men of Boma village I greet you," Tikayo said by way of an opening remark.

"We salute you too," the men chorused in reply.

"We're all aware of the calamities that has befallen Boma village, he began, "our village has known peace for a long time until this sad moments came upon us…"

"The gods of our land will get us out of this trouble," the chief priest interrupted.

"Thank you," Tikayo replied and continued despite the interruption of course he could do nothing about it after all it was the chief priest of Rorche that made the remark and not one of his wives.

"We have offered sacrifices to our God…." Tikayo said. "Yet things are not changing so one night I asked our god to tell me why this evil persisted. Then I went to sleep and I had this dream. What a dream it was," he said pausing while the men around him listened with bated breath, as if breathing normally will drown Tikayo's voice.

CHAPTER NINE

"In that dream I found myself in the market selling some form of food items and the villagers will come to my stand pick up an item and turn to pay somebody else…" Tikayo's narration was interrupted with a grunt from the men.

"Sincerely that is what happened," he maintained.

"So what did you do to arrest such a horrible development," a man asked from the crowd.

Tikayo grunted like a pig, murmured briefly to himself before responding. "Again, I was powerless I couldn't stop the people from carrying my goods and despite my protest the man receiving payment for my goods refused to give me my money… 'This money is not yours it is mine you have not done what you were supposed to do that is why this bad luck has befallen you and your business..'. That was the cold answer I got from the man who was receiving payment for my goods. Immediately I woke up from sleep," Tikayo concluded.

"What is the meaning of such a dream?" This time it was Mumba who asked the question. The answer took a while in coming.

"The ways of the gods are different from the ways of man," Tikayo was saying

"Very true," the men chorused.

"The gods do not make their ways known to any body except those who serve as oracles to the gods–here in Boma village we are lucky to have a chief priest," he said pausing for a while. "Men of Boma village I believe our chief priest having heard of my experiences has spoken with the gods and now will tell us what the Gods are saying," Tikayo concluded and sat down.

Immediately, the chief priest took over as he stood up to give the men, the interpretation of Tikayo's dream. "Men of Boma village we must be grateful to the gods because they have decided to let us into their sacred ways of operation," the chief priest said. The men held their peace by refusing to utter a word rather they were content to follow the chief priest's direction preferring to speak after he may have said his piece.

"The gods really love us men of Boma village our problem is over the moment we do what the gods wants us to do," here again the chief priest paused while surveying the faces of the men.

"What do the gods wants from us?" Mumba asked trying at the same time to hide his boredom.

"The gods have not demanded anything hard from us," the chief priest began by way of a reply. "The event in the dream as interpreted to me by the gods simply means that the gods are still angry at the fact that they had been neglected by those they were protecting."

"But we'd just offered sacrifices about three weeks ago," Kato said.

"Yes that is true but the gods feel indifferent in that the sacrifice was done out of necessity and not respect," the chief priest said before concluding. "Thus the gods feel slighted over this total disrespect by the people of Boma village." The Chief Priest said.

"Men of Boma village," Tikayo said standing up, "we must appease the gods at once," he said with absolute authority cutting off every opposition that might have risen.

"Who knows the gods having been appeased will now chase away the evil from our midst?" Deep down even as he spoke, Tikayo was amused at the whole charade.

Which evil were the gods chasing away? He was the evil and up till now the gods are yet to expose him. It said a lot about the gods they were worshipping anyway it suited his activities. At least they will continue making sacrifices while he went on with his killing.

Having arrived at the conclusion that another sacrifice was inevitable, the meeting ended on that note.

"I hope this time the killing will stop or else there will be trouble," Abokito threatened.

"Yes I agree with you," Mumba added.

Tikayo killed his next victim without delay; in fact the killing had occurred just two days after the second series of sacrifices was made to Rorche. He did not consider waiting for two weeks like in the past. His victim this time was a girl whom he had met alone on one of the village path. Killing her too was not a difficult task just like other victims. Taking out the liver and the heart, Tikayo left the body on the path he did not bother concealing it. If anything, his actions portrayed that he preferred the body be discovered and thus reducing time spent searching for missing bodies.

Furthermore, he didn't need to bother about the bodies after all he had never been challenged by any of the men in the village. He knew the penalty his actions would attract upon himself and his whole family. Should the villagers find out his sordid deeds? If Tikayo was bothered about Boma village and their laws he didn't show it. Securing his prized possessions, Tikayo rushed to the river for a quick rub down before returning home. This was intended to achieve two things, first wash off the blood stains on his body and the second thing was a routine he usually observed daily as he prepared to return home from the field with his cattle. In Boma village, the villagers had a popular saying that nine days is for the thief while the owner of the farm had just one day to catch the thief stealing his crops.

Tikayo's days were numbered but he did not know it neither did he know that from a vantage point one of the men had observed him right from the time he got to the river bank all the furtive glances he kept making while undressing. In any case, the man slipped away having concluded his business at the river. However, he resolved to get three other men and together they would start keeping surveillance on every move Tikayo made.

CHAPTER TEN

It all started like a rumour and gradually the news spread round the entire Boma village.

"What is this news I am hearing?" Abokito asked his wife.

"What is the news my master" his wife replied.

"Ah-ah, have you not heard that Romi the daughter of Ajuba is missing?" he queried.

"Say no more my master," she replied feigning surprise. Actually, she too had heard but since her husband had indicated his intention to disclose some news to her which she had suspected had to do with the disappearance of Romi she now feigned ignorance and rather allowed her husband to be the one to break the news instead of vice–versa. Coming from the men it was always a great piece of news but from the women it would be treated with contempt and dismissed as gossip or rumour. In most cases the woman could get a beating for spreading false news but if she were lucky that her husband was in a good mood she got a warning, which constituted a wagging of the finger with some stern words.

"You mean, you've not heard that Ajuba's child has been missing?" Abokito asked again.

"My master I am hearing for the first time." His wife replied.

Abokito sat silently for a while staring into space presently he came back to himself.

"There will be trouble in Boma village such that no man has ever experienced and till the killer is exposed no man in Boma village shall have his peace," he vowed with the fury of the hunter that he was. Abokito got to his feet and was on his way to the village square when he ran into Mumba and Jumbi both men were discussing in an animated manner and did not see Abokito approach.

"I greet you all," Abokito said

"The gods be praised," Mumba said on seeing him.

"Anything new" Abokito asked.

"Yes, Jumbi was just telling me what he saw today."

"What did you see?" Abokito asked. At Mumba's prompting Jumbi narrated his story for the second time.

"That's the evidence we need to bring Tikayo to book. I've always suspected that man right from the moment my son disappeared," Abokito said.

"Take it easy let us form a squad that will watch him," Jumbi counseled.

"We should not do anything rash the rope is almost finished and in no time Tikayo if he is the killer will be in our net and the whole village will know." Mumba warned.

With this wise counsel Abokito's plan to sack the chief priest was shelved. Together with three other men they formed a surveillance squad that will expose the killer and they also took an oath of silence. This was done without the knowledge of the chief and the men.

Romi's body was discovered that very evening by the men who had gone in search of her. They found her corpse lying on one of the paths that led to Boma village. Like some of the other bodies discovered too, Romi's chest had been cut open and her heart and liver were missing

"May Rorche helps us catch the doer of this evil," one of the men said. The other men chorused their agreement in the presence of all the men including Tikayo and the chief priest. Romi was buried in the bush with a prayer from her father urging her to pursue her killer and not to allow them a moment's peace.

"One day we shall know the killer of our children and wives and he will die a slow and painful death," the chief priest swore.

Dejection and desperation descended on Boma village like a heavy cloud of dew. Nobody was sure of anything again, mothers were afraid to venture out talk less of sending children to run errands. If women who were grown up could be overpowered and killed the children stood no chance at all because they were always carefree and never observant. Things got so bad that most of the men in Boma village were now running errands for their wives. No woman or child ever went out without being accompanied by the head of the family. Errands were timed to coincide with the presence of the men and as a result of this trend many families started eating their evening meals late.

While the rest of Boma village was gripped with fear the story was different in

Tikayo's house. His family members went about as if the killer related with them on first name basis. This development led to most villagers pointing accusing fingers at their chief. Tikayo was not perturbed by this development in his domain, he believed the men would get tired soon and roles will reverse again but he was in for a big surprise. The surveillance continued.

It was in the midst of the desperation and fear that Abokito and the other five men had swung into action. Their plan was a very simple one, everyday two men would quietly sneak out from the village early in the morning and would take up vantage position on the treetops. Each man covered a different path seeing the various families as they went about their chores for the day.

The men having been adequately furnished with provisions remained at the top hidden from the view of people below. The only time they ever came down was if they had to answer to the call of nature. It was risky dozing as you could fall down from the top and may likely end up with a broken limb. While the men for each day were at their point watching the remaining men took care of their chores and families. Their family members having been warned never asked questions on the whereabouts of the head of their homes.

For almost three weeks nothing changed in Boma village the men still ran errands for their families while no killing was recorded either. But the men were not fooled and they even went to the extent of warning their chief of the danger of sending his children on errand.

He laughed, "My children, nothing can happen to them," he boasted "in fact they're the only children brave enough to walk about freely in Boma village". The men realized it was useless arguing and so they left their chief alone.

It was during the tenth week of their surveillance that the mystery finally ended, and Tikayo nabbed as he attempted to kill his son. The end for Tikayo had come sooner than any of the five men thought but for

Tikayo it was no surprise, as he knew his luck would run out one day. Way into the tenth week, he had noticed that the men were holding out longer than he had anticipated and to worsen his case the desire to eat another human liver was almost consuming him. 'These men are holding much longer than I thought,' he observed. But I need liver right now, Tikayo reminded himself. Well since the women and children are protected then I will beam my searchlight inwards. By killing one of my child, I would satisfy my desire for the time being till I get another victim. Having resolved this, the die was cast. One of Tikayo's sons will pay the price so that his father will satisfy his craving for human liver. Thus that fateful morning Abokito and Mumba were already in their positions, from their vantage position they watched the various families go by including the chiefs wives and children. Then shortly Tikayo appeared with his cattle followed by one of his sons and they took the path manned by Abokito.

As the sun changed position, things change dramatically below. Tikayo had watched his son take charge of the cattle all morning while he rendered minimal assistance. Deep down the urge to get a liver was burning deep in him, lifting his eyes he observed his son's position and waited for the right time to strike. From his vantage position, Abokito watched quietly and positively hoping that things would play out accordingly thus putting an end to this surveillance business. Spending the whole day watching people move to and fro was telling on them seriously. Abokito was still lost in thoughts when he heard a cry of pain below him. Tikayo with the speed of a tiger had attacked his son intending to land the club on his head as that would have killed him instantly but he missed by inches hitting him on the back. The boy's cry of pain and surprise brought Abokito out of his reverie even as Tikayo struck again this time the blow connected and the boy remained on the ground having lost consciousness.

Abokito could not believe his eyes, "Let me wait and see what he will do next. He didn't have to wait long as Tikayo whipped out his dagger and was about to cut open his son's chest.

"At last so Tikayo is the killer," Abokito said, shocked at the scene below him. "Leave him alone," Abokito shouted from the top of the tree. Tikayo didn't think the voice was real and was beginning to cut into the boy's chest when Abokito shouted again descending from the tree at the same time. From the other path, Jumba added his voice too because from his position he had seen Tikayo attack his son. Tikayo did not bother to run for he knew he would be hunted down before the next day.

He remained rooted to the scene of the crime like a statue.

"So you're the killer?" Jumba said, as they reached Tikayo. It was more of a statement than a question.

"So what if I am the killer?" Tikayo asked defiantly as he lunged at Jumba with his dagger. But the younger man was faster he stepped out of the way and followed it with a blow that sent Tikayo crashing to the ground.

"So all along it was you," Abokito said. "You are the killer who takes away the liver of your helpless victims". Abokito asked in shock and disbelieve.

The shouts and commotion that ensued attracted the attention of villagers working in some of the farms. Tikayo despite his setbacks remained unrepentant.

"What have you all come to see?" he shouted at the villagers. The people stared at him perplexed.

"I killed them all and ate their livers and hearts and how delicious they were," he boasted.

"Kai, shut up," Udago shouted landing series of blows on his head.

"You savage, beast, evil spirit that had been tormenting Boma village, now we've caught up with you at last," Udago said, advancing forward in a menacing manner but Jumba restrained him. But more beating was still coming Tikayo's way.

"How could it be?" Mumba asked, in amazement

"Please somebody tell me it is a bad dream," Joba said but nobody answered him. The villagers gathered around Tikayo merely stared totally perplexed, overwhelmed and speechless.

"To think that it was our own chief that had been our problem.. our own chief who ate his subjects without any remorse," Abokito lamented speaking for the second time since accosting Tikayo. The men standing beside him nodded their heads in agreement

"And he was always suggesting sacrifices to Rorche," Joba added.

"Is that all?" Abokito asked. "He has been at the fore front on the need to sacrifice even going to the extent of giving the cows needed for the job to be done."

As the villagers already on the spot continued talking about what had happened, more people continued to arrive from the farms and surrounding bushes.

Not satisfied with the way things were, Abokito pushed through till he was standing face to face with Tikayo again after observing him for awhile, Abokito looked into the sky and shook his head, "No wonder we could not catch the killer," he said. "So where did you bury my son?" He asked looking down at Tikayo. There was total silence as if the people gathered stopped breathing for a while. Tikayo laughed in a deranged manner.

"Did you say your son or are you not willing to know how I killed all of them? Your son indeed why don't you go into the bush and look for him" He shouted back. Abokito responded angrily and fast, landing series of blows on Tikayo's face before the men pulled him away.

"Leave me let me deal with this cannibal," Abokito screamed as the men pulled him away.

"Don't worry the laws of our village will take care of him". Ogadi said in his baritone voice immediately the people froze Ogadi examined Tikayo carefully and hissed. "Take him to the village square" Ogadi ordered. Immediately, four able bodied men pounced on Tikayo binding his hands they brought him to the village square.

While the commotion lasted, Ntumba Tikayo's son that was rescued earlier on from being slit open by his father stirred, Ntumba had been attacked by his father who clubbed him into unconsciousness. His groaning attracted some of the villagers nearby everybody had been so engrossed with Tikayo that they forgot about him, in fact nobody paid Ntumba any attention. Thus his groaning now forced some villagers to come closer.

"The boy is about coming out of his unconsciousness" one of the villagers said.

"My head-o," Ntumba groaned, "Ahhh my back," he moaned further.

"Take it easy," another woman counseled.

"You should thank the gods for delivering you from your evil father." The woman said.

Eventually Ntumba remained on the ground and was no longer moaning. As Tikayo was about being bound to be taken to the village square, Ntumba managed to stand up and after a couple of groggy steps he stabilized a bit. Quietly and gently Ntumba made his way to the farm to inform the entire family of the latest events in Boma village.

CHAPTER ELEVEN

Tikayo's wives and children walking as fast as their legs could carry them arrived the outskirts of the village just as Ogadi and the men entered the village square with their fallen chief. Mako Tikayo's first wife and the rest of the family were already aware of the sad and despicable event that had taken place through Ntumba who had managed to reach the farm.

"I can't believe it," Mako said muttering over and over.

"This is a bad dream," Akko added. On being rescued from the clutches of his liver crazy father, Ntumba on regaining consciousness had managed to find his way to the farm where his mother and other members of the family were sweating it out under the hot sun. His mother was surprised to see him, "what is it, where is your father?" Akko asked in quick succession.

Ntumba merely fell on the ground and started weeping uncontrollably and holding his head.

Okanu moved to where he lay, "what is the matter," he asked just as Teoki joined him. Akko was astonished and beside herself with anxiety. Ntumba's wailing attracted the attention of the first wife as well as the rest of the children who now joined Teoki and Okanu and were making spirited attempts to know why Ntumba was weeping.

"What is wrong with you? "Mako asked gently bending down to examine his legs for snakebites or scorpion stings. As the first wife, she was mother to all the children in the family.

"Ntumba why are you refusing to tell us what is disturbing you now? "Akko pleaded looking very worried. "Did your father beat you or is he in trouble?"

Suddenly Mako cried out, "what is this?" she asked massaging the bump on Ntumba's head gently.

"It was father who hit me with a big stick, first on the back and then on the head.."

"Why did he hit you with a big stick?" Akko probed further interrupting.

The two women were amazed and exchanged quick worried glances with one another.

"Tell us now what did you do to warrant his hitting you with a big stick," Mako continued with the questioning. Both women believed that given the naughtiness of children Ntumba must have offended his father. But when Ntumba opened up and told the story of how his father was about to kill him but for the intervention of two men who it appeared were doing something at the tree top and thus were able to see what transpired below. Of course, there was no way Ntumba would have known that it was a vigilante group that had just saved him.

"Look at my chest," Ntumba said opening his dress to reveal knife marks.

Suddenly the puzzle fell into place. "So our husband was the killer?" Mako asked in amazement, "children gather your things and let's go home immediately something bad has happened," she announced.

"May the gods protect us from the anger of the people," Akko prayed as she gathered her things. "To think that he was the killer– killing all these helpless victims…"

"Don't just stand there and lament, think of yourself and the children." Mako said harshly.

"But mother," Akko began then hesitated,

"Yes speak out," Mako ordered.

"Are you sure it's really true and not a fabrication by Ntumba?" Akko asked.

"Stay there and deceive yourself our husband is the killer. He could not get his mysterious liver again, so he now decided to turn inward and kill his own children so as to eat their liver," Mako said, while her hands continued to work at a feverish pace gathering foodstuff.

"If not for the men up the tree, Ntumba would be dead by now…"

"May the gods forbid that my child be eaten by a savage," Akko shouted also interrupting Mako. "What a life," Akko continued stunned. "Killing children, women then taking their livers and hearts home to be used as meat in his meals..".

"Are you still standing there and reflecting on nothing?" Mako asked interrupting her.

"Okay stand there as if you don't know what the villagers can do to us due to the horrible crime committed by our husband". Without further delay Mako gathered her things and all the children and they departed for the village. Of course Akko would not be left behind, she followed immediately.

As they all trudged on towards Boma village, Mako continued to go over her plans again and again. "How can I live in this village, all my life with this type of shame and stigma," she wondered aloud.

"May Rorche deliver us out of this abomination and shame" Akko prayed.

"Me? Not me..ooo" Mako said crossing her head with her hand. "Live in this village? So that the women will point at me with their left hand and say this is the woman whose husband ate my child's liver – not me," Mako stated.

"Mother what do we do now?" Akko asked.

"I don't know about you. But for me I'm leaving the village tonight" she declared emphatically.

Mother, we shall all go with you," Ntumba said.

"Yes-o," Okanu added.

"I will follow too," Teoki said. The die was cast, it was obvious that they were fleeing Boma village.

"The shame and stigma was unbearable and you could not trust these men in Boma village". Akko reflected and being aware of all these setbacks did not need any body to convince her to flee the village with her children and whatever belongings they could gather. Away from Boma village they would all start life afresh and put this ugly incident behind them forever.

CHAPTER TWELVE

The village square was a beehive of activity that afternoon. For once the men, women and children mingled freely as they all pressed to catch a glimpse of the man that had wrecked havoc on the village he was supposed to head. At this time the news had reached almost every corner.

"Ahh… now the siege is truly over we can go back to our lives," Jumbi said patting Mumba on the back.

"I feel like taking revenge" Mumba said.

Jumbi smiled, "I understand – but that won't be necessary."

Suddenly there was commotion as out of nowhere Halima, Uriji's mother and three other women suddenly appeared and pushed their way to where Tikayo sat.

"Behold the killer of my son," Halima announced and immediately pounced on the former chief biting, scratching and raining abuses on him. The other women followed suit. Tikayo was spared further brutalization by Ogadi who chased the women away.

Tension and excitement mixed freely as the people continued to talk at the same time with no one really making sense except you were really close to somebody.

"No wonder he was so non-chalant the day my son disappeared and I came to report to him," Abokito's wife now opened up.

"Really?" Halima asked, "Well as for me.. o, I've just dealt with him too. But tell me how you mean that he was non-chalant to you". Halima probed further.

"Hmmm," Abokito's wife began. Then went on to narrate all that happened the day her son vanished without a trace.

"And you did not report to your husband?" Halima asked with eyes ablaze.

"I did, but my husband merely dismissed it as a trick of my imagination," Abokito's wife replied.

"Wooo, wonders will never cease," Halima exclaimed.

"But you know men," Abokito's wife began. "All along he had a plan with some other men which we did not know about till now, but now we can see the results," she concluded.

"Anyway I thank the gods for this revelation," Halima added.

Suddenly, the excitement rose among the people gathered in the village square as the chief priest flanked by his assistant entered the village square. Taking his usual position the chief priest raised his flywhisk and there was silence.

"People of Boma village I greet you." The people responded with enthusiasm and waited again for his next line of action.

"People of Boma village, I greet you all" the chief priest hailed.

"I greet you all in the name of Rorche – our god that has done great things for all of us in this village…" The chief priest went on and on in his narration of events in the past "…But today our god has come to our rescue," he said.

"Which god?" Abokito remarked to his friends around him.

"The God that could not save us despite our sacrifices? It is due to our own strength that we were able to apprehend this killer."

His friends prevailed on him to calm down.

"At least we have caught him, maybe he will die by hanging or will be banished to the evil forest to die there unmourned," Mumba said.

They all lapsed into silence and focused their attention on the chief priest who was still talking.

"Well people of Boma village, now we have seen with our own eyes that it was our own chief that had all along been killing our wives and children also taking out their livers and most time their hearts. All in the urge to satisfy his craving for liver," the chief priest paused.

"But how did it all begin?" a villager asked from the crowd.

"I won't go over the whole story again, let us be satisfied that a mysterious liver caused this problem," the chief priest said by way of an answer. While he spoke Tikayo hands bound and flanked by two guards watched quietly without any expression on his face as the village decided his fate. "We all know the laws guiding us in this village," the chief priest was saying. He reminded the people of the fact that the chief priest was the custodian of the laws but in executing them there were cases the entire village had to meet such as the case at hand. "Tikayo's offence was an abomination beyond description. In Boma village, killing a fellow man would turn you into an outcast and of course nobody in his right senses would associate with such a person. But to kill in the brutish manner that Tikayo did was the worst evil ever to befall Boma village…" the chief priest paused. "But Boma village has severe punitive measures and the penalty for killing in this manner was banishment into the evil forest where the culprit would wonder about till he dies. If during the period of banishment he is caught in any of the villages he would be put to death. The second form of punishment was death by hanging however the decision will be reached by the people as our own laws stipulates." the chief priest said.

There was some grumbling and murmuring from the crowd.

"However nobody would hurt his family," the chief priest was saying. "And the family members will be free to go about their businesses but the land will be cleansed of the evil that has been done".

But in the case of Tikayo's family, his first wife had her own plans.

Boma village could go on with its laws but as far as she was concerned they were fleeing the village. The chief priest surveyed the faces of the village elders as well as the villagers suddenly he turned to face the fallen head of Boma village

"Tikayo what you did is an abomination to this village and the land must be cleansed of this evil" he pointed out. Meanwhile the villagers held their breath and waited as the moment of decision was at hand.

"People of Boma village it is time to decide the fate of the evil one in our midst," the chief priest announced.

"Kill him," Halima shouted from the front of the crowd.

"Make way," Mumba said pushing his way forward. Coming face to face with the chief priest and elders he stopped.

"This man," he said pointing at Tikayo, "killed our children and wives because he wanted to satisfy his craving for liver. He caused misery and sorrow to many homes, it is only natural that he should be paid back with the same coin," he paused. "I believe his family should be brought here to see their father die". Mumba's statement drew sharp responses from the crowd, some villagers agreed with Mumba's view while others disagreed. Many other men including Jumbi and Abokito came forward and added their views that Tikayo be taken out of the village and hung on a tree till he dies. A serious argument raged among the villagers, many argued that he should be banished into the evil forest to die there. But another group maintained that hanging him was a better option more so as he had a very terrible reputation as a cannibal and a killer if banished he could start preying on the village thereby causing more harm. Meanwhile Tikayo watched speechlessly as his subjects decided his fate.

"Where is Tikayo's family? "The chief priest asked suddenly.

"If there are not here then they would be at home." Ogadi replied.

"Please dispatch two men to confirm for us." The chief priest requested.

Without delay Mumba and Jumbi were picked and sent to Tikayo's compound to check on his family members. The proceedings once again refocused on the issue at stake. With the villagers expressing a divided opinion, a separation was done and those villagers who wanted Tikayo to die by hanging carried the day so Tikayo's fate was sealed that afternoon.

Shortly before making the official pronouncement the two men sent earlier on returned from their mission and reported to Ogadi who in turn whispered something to the chief priest.

"Tikayo after due consultation with the men and women of Boma village and the elders you've been found guilty of a very terrible abomination and you are to die by hanging," the chief priest announced.

Suddenly Udago pushed forward, "What about his family members?" he asked.

"I do not think it is fair that they should be allowed to go free," Udago concluded.

"Udago I believe you've got ears and you must have heard that the family members are to be left alone," Ogadi fired back. Udago retreated quietly into the crowd.

"For your information, Tikayo's family has fled the village. I hope you are satisfied now?" The chief priest queried. At the mention of his family Tikayo suddenly sat up but nobody answered him.

"Let us not bring the wrath of the gods upon us. Tikayo is the culprit not his family members. Should you meet them anywhere I strongly advise that no harm befalls them. May Rorche continue to protect and guide us."

The chief priest and the villagers made their exit from the village square while Tikayo was led away to his death.

EPILOGUE

Tikayo was executed very early in the morning. The women were barred from going to the execution site only the men were given the privilege of watching their fallen chief face the gallows. He was taken out of the hut where he was kept as a prisoner to the fringes of the forest and hanged on a big baobab tree. As for his family members, since they had fled to an unknown destination nobody bothered about them any more.

But this development coupled with their dissatisfaction over the whole episode took a new turn as irate villagers sneaked into Tikayo's compound setting it on fire, they watched delightfully as the compound burned to the ground having divided his cattle among themselves.

The elders of Boma village never made any enquiries. After all it was a cleansing process.

With Tikayo dead, his family gone and his compound burnt to the ground, Boma village once again began to enjoy peace and tranquility.

ABOUT THE AUTHOR

Mike Effa was born in Cross River State, after a brief stint in the newspaper business he proceeded to the University of Calabar where he obtained a bachelors degree in Adult Education/Political science.
Mike served in Kano with the Ado Bayero University. He worked with Nigeria Conscience Media Ltd as Deputy Editor.

A gifted Writer, Mike's first novel titled **"The Man Without a Backbone"** published by West African Books publishers, Lagos-Nigeria is currently on sales worldwide.

His hobbies include reading, writing, dxing, and football. Mike Effa is an Assistant Chief Admin Officer with the Nigeria Natural Medicine Development Agency in Lagos, Nigeria

Mike Effa lives in Lagos with his wife- Bola and son - Asher.

Imaginarium Self-Publishing

An Imprint of Copyhouse Press London

Lightning Source UK Ltd.
Milton Keynes UK
UKOW02f0001090316

269875UK00003B/231/P